D0316182

Georgie
the Royal Prince Fairy

LIBRARIES NI
WITHDRAWN FROM STOCK

Daisy Meadows

ORCHARD

www.rainbowmagic.co.uk

Story One
The Royal Weekend

Chapter One

Best Friends Fun

"Rachel, are you awake?" whispered Kirsty Tate.

It was early on a Saturday morning. Rachel was staying at Kirsty's house, and it was the start of a very special weekend!

"Yes, I'm too excited to sleep!" Rachel Walker replied.

"Can you believe we're going to see three real princes today?"

"And we're going to meet them at the palace garden party tomorrow," added Kirsty with a smile.

Rachel hopped out of bed and opened the curtains. The summer sun was already shining outside. She climbed into bed beside her best friend.

The whole country was excited about the royal weekend. The Queen had invited three royal princes from other countries to stay for the weekend. They were going to launch a new ship and watch a special horse race. Lots of children had been invited to a special children's garden party at the palace, including Rachel and Kirsty!

Wetherbury was close to the palace, so Rachel and her parents were staying with the Tate family for the whole weekend.

"It's going to be a busy day," said Kirsty. "Mum said we have to leave early to make sure we get a good view of the ship launch."

"Yes, and then we have to catch the train to the racecourse," Rachel remembered.

Just then, Kirsty gave Rachel a gentle nudge with her elbow, and pointed at her bedside table.

There was Kirsty's tiara.

It was only made of plastic, but now it was glimmering as if it were made of real diamonds.

"That looks like fairy magic!" cried Rachel, with a great big smile.

Chapter Two

Georgie the Royal Prince Fairy

The girls heard a tiny laugh, and a beautiful fairy appeared next to the tiara. She twirled across the bedside table and curtsied.

"Hello, Rachel and Kirsty," she said. "I'm Georgie the Royal Prince Fairy."

The best friends smiled happily. A visit from a fairy made the weekend absolutely perfect! Kirsty and Rachel had been friends of Fairyland for a long time, and had met lots of wonderful fairy friends.

"Hello, Georgie!" the girls said. "It's lovely to meet you."

"I'm very happy to meet you both at last," said Georgie. She fluttered over to perch on Kirsty's bed. She was wearing a pretty polka-dot dress and sparkling shoes. A golden tiara

was tucked into her shining
blonde hair.

"I look after all princes in
the fairy and human worlds,"
Georgie explained to the girls.
"I'm here today to give you a
special invitation."

She flicked her wand and a
magical scroll appeared in the
air. Golden writing began to
appear on the scroll.

Dear Rachel and Kirsty,
Princess Grace and Prince
Arthur are proud to announce
the birth of their son. You are
invited to celebrate with them
on Sunday at the royal
naming ceremony.

The girls gave gasps
of delight. "That sounds
wonderful!" said Kirsty.
"We'd love to come!" added
Rachel with a beaming smile.
Suddenly, Kirsty had a
horrible thought.

"What about Jack Frost?" she asked. "I bet he'll try to ruin the ceremony!"

Georgie smiled. "Don't worry, Kirsty," she said. "It will all be fine. The Ice Lord is coming to the ceremony, and has promised to be on his best behaviour."

Kirsty still felt a bit worried. After all, mean Jack Frost could not be trusted!

"I'll come and collect you on Sunday afternoon, after the garden party at the palace," said Georgie.

"We're really looking forward to it," Rachel replied. "Thank you very much for bringing the invitation!"

Georgie gave them a little wave. Then she disappeared in a flurry of tiny, glittering crowns. Rachel and Kirsty looked at each other.

"This is going to be the best weekend ever!" said Rachel.

The best friends jumped out of bed and started to get ready for the day.

But a moment later, Georgie appeared on the bedside table again. This time, she wasn't smiling and her cheeks were pale.

"Oh, girls, something awful has happened," she cried. "While I was visiting you, Jack Frost stole my special royal seal!"

"Oh no!" said Kirsty. "But what exactly is the royal seal?"

"It's a golden ring with a special pattern engraved on it," Georgie explained. "It's an important part of all naming ceremonies for princes, because I use it as a stamp to complete the naming certificate."

The pretty little fairy put her head in her hands. "If we don't find the royal seal soon, the naming ceremony will be cancelled, and the newborn prince won't have a name!"

Rachel and Kirsty looked at each other, horrified.

"We know that Jack Frost is hiding in the human world," said Georgie. "And the royal seal is drawn towards royalty, so Jack Frost will probably be close to the visiting princes."

"We'll help you to look for Jack Frost and the seal," said Rachel. "The princes will be at the ship launch this morning."

Just then, there was a tap on the door. Georgie hid under Kirsty's hair. Mrs Tate popped her head around the door and smiled at them.

"Good morning," she said.  "Come and have your breakfast, and then we'll set off to see the ship launch."

The girls hurried downstairs after Kirsty's mum. They had a very busy day ahead!

Story Two

Royal Rescues

Chapter One

Making a Splash

When Rachel and Kirsty got
to the docks, there were lots of
people everywhere. Everyone
was having lots of fun! Georgie
sat on Kirsty's shoulder, hidden
by her hair.

A loudspeaker system suddenly
crackled into life. "It's time for a

marching display by the ship's crew!" a voice announced.

The crew marched out into the area in front of Rachel and Kirsty. The men and women looked very smart ... all except one. His uniform was crumpled, and he kept tripping the others up.

Kirsty nudged Rachel. "I think that's a goblin!" she whispered.

Rachel nodded.

Kirsty felt Georgie squeeze her shoulder. "He could be carrying the ring for Jack Frost!" she exclaimed.

Just then, the cheers of the crowd became louder. Prince

Alexander, Prince William and Prince Louis had arrived! They all looked very smart.

Rachel saw the goblin scampering towards the platform, where the princes would stand to launch the ship. Rachel and Kirsty slipped under the barrier and chased the little goblin up the steps.

When they all reached the top, they saw the goblin pick up a big bottle of champagne, which was tied to a long piece of rope.

"That's the bottle they smash against the side of the ship to launch it," whispered Rachel.

"He's untying the rope!" Kirsty gasped. "Hey, STOP!" Georgie shot out from under

Kirsty's hair. She zoomed towards the goblin, and with a cry of alarm he fell into the sea!

Georgie waved her wand and gave the goblin a lifebelt. He floated over to some steps at the side of the docks and climbed out, dripping with water.

He stomped off angrily.

The loudspeakers crackled again. "The launch ceremony is about to start," announced the voice.

Rachel and Kirsty hurried back as the princes climbed on to the platform.

Prince Alexander picked up the bottle and swung it against the side of the ship. SMASH! Champagne foamed over the big ship. It slid down the slipway and splashed safely into the water.

Rachel and Kirsty shared
a happy smile. Next it was time
to go to Hatling Racecourse.
But would they find Georgie's
magic seal there?

Chapter Two

Horse Help

At the racecourse, Rachel and Kirsty went to watch the horses walking around the paddock before the royal race.

A dark-brown stallion was being paraded past. He had a silvery mark on his forehead, in the shape of a tiny star.

"I think that's Silver Blaze, the Queen's horse," said Kirsty.

"Oh, I hope he wins the race," said Rachel. "It would be wonderful for the princes to see a royal horse win!"

The girls knew that the princes would be watching from the Royal Box.

Soon the jockeys mounted the horses and rode up to the starting posts. Rachel and Kirsty followed them.

Rachel pointed at a brown stallion called Snowball and a grey mare called Icicle. "The jockeys riding those horses are tiny!" she said. Then she spotted that the figures had very long noses ...

"Kirsty," said Rachel in a worried voice. "I think those are goblin jockeys!"

Just then Georgie appeared. She had been hiding in a large flowery hat! The girls explained about the jockeys.

"This is bad," Georgie said.

"The goblins must be here to ruin the race. We have to stop them!"

Kirsty thought for a moment. "Georgie, could you give us the ability to talk to horses for a short time? Perhaps if we can talk to the goblins' horses, they'll be able to help us save the race."

Georgie nodded and waved her wand. Fairy dust showered the girls. They felt themselves shrinking, and shimmering wings appeared on their backs!

"Let's go!" said Rachel.

They zoomed over to the
starting gates. Rachel dived
into Snowball's brown mane,
while Kirsty tucked herself next
to Icicle's grey ear.

"Listen," Kirsty whispered.

"I'm a fairy. Your jockey is a naughty goblin, and he's going to try to spoil the race."

"Goblin?" whinnied Icicle in alarm. "Help!"

"It's OK," said Kirsty. "You just have to refuse to do anything your jockey says."

"But I always do what the jockey says," replied Icicle. "I don't know if I can race by myself!"

"Of course you can," said Kirsty in a firm voice.

"Will you stay with me?" Icicle asked.

Kirsty agreed. She had to make sure that the race went well! An official raised the starting flag.

"We'll be off any minute now," said Icicle. "Ready? Then hold on tight!"

Chapter Three

The Royal Race

In the next stall, Rachel
was finding it hard to make
Snowball listen to her!

"Your jockey is a goblin!"
cried Rachel.

"I don't even need a jockey,
I'm so good at racing,"

Snowball boasted.

"You're absolutely right," said Rachel quickly. "You should do exactly what you want, and show the princes how wonderful you are!"

Just then, the starting flag swooshed down, the stalls crashed open and the royal race began!

Rachel and Kirsty both hung on as tightly as they could to their horses' manes.

Around the first bend, Icicle's goblin rider tugged on her reins to make her go the wrong way, but she ignored him.

At the second bend, Snowball's goblin dug in his heels to make him turn sideways, but Snowball took no notice.

"Stop running!" Kirsty heard Icicle's goblin jockey yell.

"Let me off!" wailed Snowball's goblin jockey. "I feel sick!"

As they drew closer to the finish line, Snowball and Silver Blaze were right next to each other.

Just then, Rachel saw Prince
William stand up and shout
Silver Blaze's name.

The Queen's horse galloped
even faster and crossed the
finish line in first place!

The crowds went completely
wild, cheering loudly in delight.

The princes jumped out of their
seats and clapped their hands.

"Well done, you two!" said
Georgie, fluttering over to
join them. "The princes had a
wonderful time."

"I'm afraid the goblins didn't enjoy themselves," smiled Kirsty.

They watched as the goblin jockeys slithered down to the ground and walked away on wobbly legs.

"We didn't get the chance to check if they were carrying the seal," cried Rachel.

"That's what I came to tell you," said Georgie. "Queen Titania has used her magic to find out that Jack Frost has the seal!"

"Then we have to find him," said Kirsty with a gulp.

"Right now you have to return to normal size and find your parents," said Georgie.

"But I'll see you tomorrow at the palace garden party. It might be the best place to look for the royal seal!"

Story Three

Palace Parties

Chapter One

Frost in a Frock!

The next day, Mr and Mrs Tate dropped Rachel and Kirsty off at the palace for the garden party. They were really excited!

A guard wearing a tall, furry hat and a smart uniform led the girls to the gardens.

"I bet those hats get really hot on sunny days," whispered Kirsty.

Rachel gave a squeak of surprise. Georgie was peeping out from under the back of the hat!

She fluttered over to the girls and tucked herself into Rachel's shoulder bag.

"This is the last special event for the princes," said Georgie.

"I'm sure Jack Frost will be here with the royal seal."

The guard led them into the palace gardens. There were children everywhere! Waiters and waitresses were walking around the garden

with snacks and drinks. Rachel and Kirsty each took a glass of orange juice and a scone with jam and cream.

"Look over there," said Rachel. "The princes are having scones too."

The princes were sitting at a small round table nearby.

"That person looks interested in them," said Kirsty, pointing.

Someone wearing a long, flowery dress was sitting quietly on a bench under a tall tree, gazing at the princes.

Two big bony feet
stuck out from
under the dress.

"I recognise
those feet," said
Rachel in
a low voice.
"Kirsty, I'm
sure that's Jack
Frost!"

The girls slipped behind
the tree. Just then, three short
guests wearing large hats came
hurrying up to Jack Frost.

"Goblins!" said Georgie,

popping her head out of
Rachel's bag.

"Do we still have to wear
these dresses?" one of the
goblins complained.

"Yes," Jack Frost snapped.

"Now get out of my way.
I can't see the princes! How am
I supposed to learn how to be
royal without watching them?"

The goblins raced off,
bumping into tables and
sending cakes and drinks flying
through the air.

Rachel spotted something
glittering on Jack Frost's finger.
Georgie gave a squeak of
excitement. "It's the royal seal!"
she whispered.

Chapter Two

Goblins!

"We need to trick Jack Frost into giving the seal to us," said Rachel. "I think I've got an idea. Georgie, can you dress us up like the Queen's guards and give us a security scanner?"

Georgie waved her wand.

The girls found themselves in uniform and each wearing a large, furry hat, just like the guards. Rachel was holding a scanner, which looked a bit like a large phone.

The girls walked around the tree and tapped Jack Frost on the shoulder.

"We are doing a security check," said Kirsty. "We need to scan you. Follow us."

Jack Frost looked a bit cross, but he followed the girls to a quiet part of the garden.

Rachel swept the scanner over him, and it made a large beep.

Jack Frost jumped, and Rachel had to stifle a giggle.

"Please take off any metal items," she said.

"Why?" Jack Frost demanded.

"Because if you don't, we will ask you to leave the garden party," Kirsty said firmly.

Grumbling, Jack Frost pulled the royal seal off his finger. Rachel held out her hand, and Jack Frost dropped the ring into it.

Instantly, Georgie zoomed to Rachel's side and took the ring, returning it to fairy-size. The girls' disguises disappeared, and Jack Frost's mouth fell open.

"You tricksy girls!" he bellowed. "I'll make you sorry!

Goblins, get them!"

"Oh no you don't!" said Georgie. With a wave of her wand, a thorny bush sprang up around the goblins.

"Use your magic to go back to the Ice Castle," she said. "Take the goblins with you!"

Jack Frost was too angry to speak. Glaring at Georgie, he disappeared in a flash of blue lightning with his goblins.

Rachel and Kirsty shared a hug, and Georgie did a somersault in the air. Then they heard a very familiar voice behind them.

"I don't remember having a thorn bush in my garden."

It was the Queen!

Chapter Three

The Perfect Prince

The Queen was wearing a sparkly necklace and a smart dress. The girls curtseyed, and Rachel cleared her throat.

"Thorn bushes grow quickly, Your Majesty," she said.

"Maybe you've never noticed it before."

The Queen gave a little smile. "Perhaps. Well, I will leave you to explore the gardens," she said. The girls curtseyed again. When they looked up, the Queen had gone. Georgie fluttered over to them.

"Now we can hold the naming ceremony," she cried.

Sparkles of fairy dust sprinkled down on Rachel and Kirsty. The garden around them faded, and the next instant they were standing in the throne room of the Fairyland Palace!

Rachel and Kirsty gazed around in delight. The room was packed with fairies.

The king and queen were sitting on their thrones, and Prince Arthur and Princess Grace were standing beside them. To one side was a beautiful crib with blue drapes and a bow.

Queen Titania began to speak. "Now that Rachel and Kirsty have saved the royal seal, we can begin," she said. "We are here today to welcome a new and very special fairy. I am delighted to present … Prince George!"

Everyone cheered and clapped.

Just then, the door banged open and Jack Frost stomped in, frowning. He sat down and folded his arms across his chest.

"I think he's had enough of royalty!" said Rachel with a giggle.

King Oberon held up a large scroll. "This is Prince George's naming certificate," he said. "Georgie the Royal Prince Fairy, please will you stamp it with your royal seal?"

Georgie pressed the royal
seal against the certificate, and
it left a dazzling golden mark.
Everyone cheered!

Rachel and Kirsty tiptoed
over to the royal crib. The tiny

prince was fast asleep, and his gauzy blue wings were folded around his little body.

"Isn't it amazing to think that we've helped to welcome him into the world?" asked Kirsty, squeezing her best friend's hand.

Rachel nodded and smiled. "Those visiting princes have a very exciting life," she said. "But I wouldn't swap places with them for the world!"

The End

**If you enjoyed this story,
you may want to read**

Catherine the Fashion Princess Fairy
Early Reader

Here's how the story begins ...

"Three cheers for the princesses!" shouted an excited tourist.

Outside the royal gates, Rachel Walker and Kirsty Tate cheered along with the rest of the crowd, and then gazed up at the palace in the heart of the city.

The elegant, spiral railings outside were painted gold, and decorated with tiny silver hummingbirds.

"Isn't it amazing to think that your mum's friend is in there right now, talking to the youngest princess?" said Rachel to her best friend.

Kirsty nodded. Everyone loved the three princesses, but the youngest – Princess Edie – was their favourite.

"I wonder which room is hers," she said.

"I think it's that one," said Rachel, pointing up at an open window where long white curtains were billowing in the summer breeze.

Read
Catherine the Fashion Princess
Early Reader
to find out
what happens next!